Bubbit

MAGGiE SmiTH

Clarion Books

Houghton Mifflin Harcourt

Boston x New York

I have a bunny—he's made of soft wool fabric. He has silky ears, a fluffy tail, and a special row of X's on his foot.

My bunny's name is Bubbit, and he's almost just my age. That's because my grandma Nonni made him for me way back when I was teeny-tiny.

My Nonni can sew anything, and I love everything
she makes, but Bubbit is her number-one creation.

When I feel mad, he helps calm me down.
When I feel sad, he helps cheer me up.
He's a very special bunny.

Nonni says Bubbit was made with love and stuffed with a thousand kisses. That's what his special row of X's means. I can feel it in the dark.

I love sewing too. Nonni sent me my own sewing basket,
with my own tomato pincushion, so that someday I can be
like her. Then I'll make a whole zoo full of friends for Bubbit.
I practice my stitches almost every day.

Since Bubbit and I are practically twins, we always understand each other. When we found out there was going to be a new baby, we weren't sure we *wanted* a new baby.

But now we are excited.
We're making a picture to welcome the new baby.
Bubbit says it needs more blue.
If you say so, Bubbit!

Nonni's here to stay with us for two whole weeks!
She smells like lemon candies,
and she's wearing her blue skirt—
the one that matches Bubbit.

When I'm helping her unpack, I find her sewing basket.
"Are we going to make something?" I ask.
"I hope so," says Nonni. "We'll have lots of time together."

Today Nonni took Bubbit and me to the hospital.

I have a new baby brother!
His ears stick out like Daddy's, and his hands
are teeny-weeny. You can practically see through his fingers!

I got to hold him, and he didn't even cry.
Bubbit agreed that he seemed like a pretty good baby.

"Let's make the baby a present!" I say when we get home.
"Good idea," says Nonni. "What should it be?"

We look in his room—at his tiny clothes,
the bird mobile, and the old rocking chair.

When we look at his crib, Bubbit whispers in my ear.
"What is it?" Nonni asks.

"He says it looks lonely in there," I say.
"Oh, dear," says Nonni. "What should we do?"

Bubbit whispers in my ear again.
"That's it!" I say.
"We need to make the baby his own special friend—
a friend like Bubbit, who will always be there."

"You mean another bunny?" Nonni asks.
"No way!" I say. "Bubbit is the only bunny."
"Then what?" Nonni asks.

Just then, Bubbit
looks at the door, and
I know what he means.
"An elephant!" I say.
"Yay!"

Nonni stares hard at my elephant. Then we get to work.
Nonni scribbles and draws and erases. She thinks and
measures and *Hmm*s. When the pattern is ready,
Bubbit and I help cut out the shapes.

Then we need fabric.

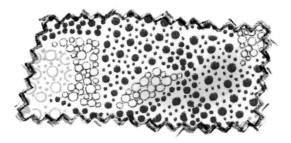

We look through the scrap basket, but nothing is right.

"We could choose another color," Nonni says.

But Bubbit wants yellow.

Then I remember . . . my old favorite jacket,
the one that Nonni made. It is soft corduroy, and
I love it very much. But now it is way too small for me.

"Are you sure?" Nonni asks.

I am sure. Bubbit and I help Nonni cut apart my old jacket.
"There's a lot of good material here," Nonni says.

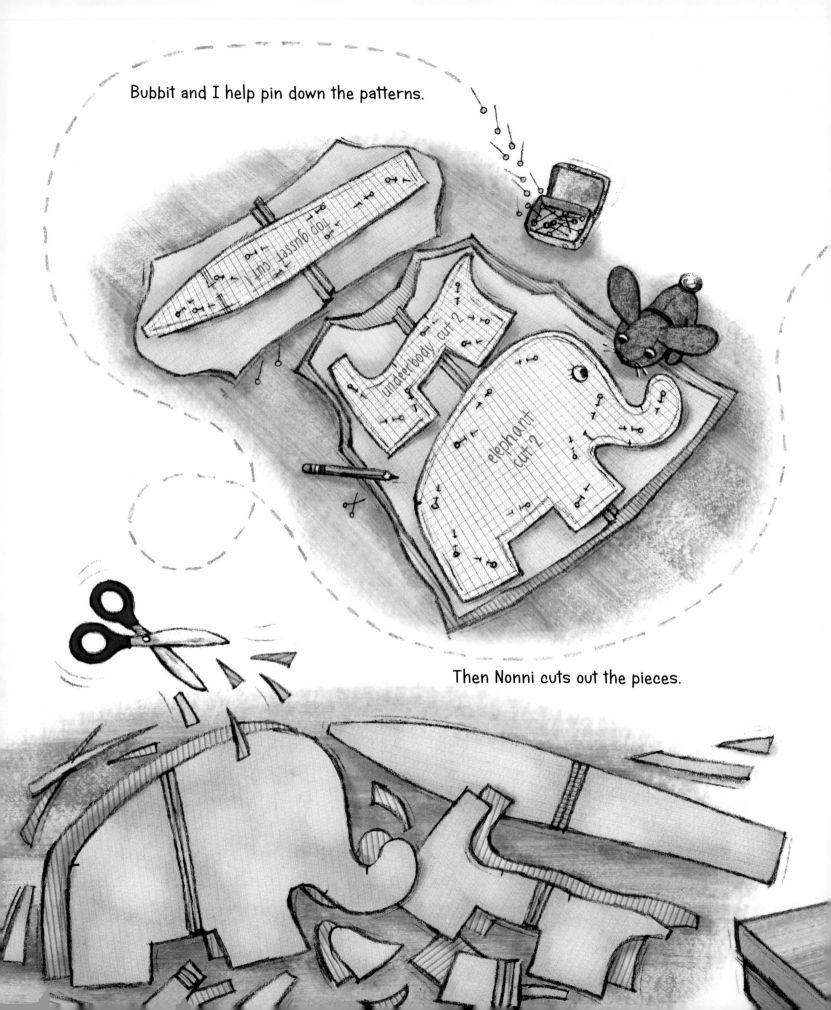

Bubbit and I help pin down the patterns.

Then Nonni cuts out the pieces.

Bubbit and I help pin the pieces together. Then Nonni sews them on Mommy's old sewing machine. *Whir, whir,* it goes. Nonni sews fast! She puts pins in her mouth, but I'm not allowed to until I'm big.

Cut and pin,

pin and sew.

We want something different for the
ears and feet. Bubbit looks in the scrap
basket and finds the perfect thing.
It's soft and thick, and it feels
like a blanket.

"The baby will like this,"
Nonni says. We cut out
two ears and four feet.

I get to make my own
stitches on the ears,
just for decoration.

It's looking more
like an elephant, but
something is missing.
Stuffing!

We stuff small bits at a time so there won't be lumps.
"Don't forget the kisses!" I say.

We take turns blowing them in, until there are more than a thousand.

Then Nonni sews everything closed so the kisses won't fall out.

Cut and pin,

pin and sew,

pin and sew and snip!

We make eyes out of felt, and
a braided tail out of yarn.

Then Nonni sews them onto the elephant.

Now it's time for the special row
of X's, just like the one Bubbit has.
When he gets big enough, I'll tell
my little brother what it means.

I think we're all done,
but Bubbit whispers in my ear.
"You're right," I say.

Then we get my ribbon box.

"Perfect!" Nonni says.
"Hooray!" I say.

"That was a lot of work," Nonni says, stretching her back.
"Yes, it was," I agree, "but look what we made!"

After supper, we read books until bedtime.
Bubbit chooses all of his favorites.
"Good job today," Nonni says.
"You did most of it," I say, "but I'm learning."

"Guess what?" Nonni asks.
"What?" I wonder.
"You're going to be a *super* big sister."
"Really?" I say. "How do you know?"
"Because," Nonni answers, "some things I just know."

And I just know that my new baby brother
will love his big corduroy elephant...

just as much as I love
my blue wool bunny, Bubbit.

In my

pincushion

scissors

thread

pins

needle threader

needles

measuring tape

pencil

sewing basket:

seam ripper

53 54 55 56 57 58 59

thimble

rick rack

safety pins

snaps

embroidery floss

felt for practicing

buttons

My Blue Bunny,

For budding sewists everywhere

Clarion Books ✘ 215 Park Avenue South, New York, New York 10003 ✘ Copyright © 2014 by Maggie Smith
All rights reserved. ✘ For information about permission to reproduce selections from this book, write to Permissions,
Houghton Mifflin Harcourt Publishing Company, 215 Park Avenue South, New York, New York 10003. ✘ Clarion Books is an imprint of
Houghton Mifflin Harcourt Publishing Company. ✘ www.hmhbooks.com ✘ The illustrations were executed in pencil, fabric, and painted papers,
assembled digitally. ✘ The text was set in Candy Round. ✘ Library of Congress Cataloging-in-Publication Data ✘ Smith, Maggie,
1965– author, illustrator. ✘ My blue bunny, Bubbit / by Maggie Smith. ✘ pages cm ✘ Summary: A little girl who loves her blue wool bunny
makes a special toy friend for her new baby brother. ✘ ISBN 978-0-547-55861-5 (hardcover) ✘ [1. Brothers and sisters—Fiction.
2. Babies—Fiction. 3. Toys—Fiction.] I. Title. ✘ PZ7.S65474Mv 2013 ✘ [E]—dc23 ✘ 2012046024 ✘ Manufactured in China
SCP 10 9 8 7 6 5 4 3 2 1 ✘ 4500436458